A MAN IS JUST FLESH-AND-BLOOD, AND

CAN BE IGNORED OR DESTROYED.

BUT A SYMBOL... AS A SYMBOL
I CAN BE INCORRUPTIBLE,

BATMAN BEGINS

THE OFFICIAL MOVIE GUIDE

text by **Claudia Kalindjian**

images courtesy of **Warner Bros.**

design by **John J. Hill**

screenplay by **Christopher Nolan** and **David S. Goyer**
story by **David S. Goyer**

Batman created by **Bob Kane**

EVERLASTING . . .

FOREWORD

Set out to make a Batman film, and you're instantly immersed in a kaleidoscope of images and possibilities: everything the character has ever been portrayed in from the thousands of comic book stories to hundreds of animated television episodes to the half-dozen previous films and on; and everything that hasn't yet been done with one of the most versatile characters to emerge from the human imagination. What can Gotham City be, as a city that is itself a character in the Batman stories? What lurks beneath Wayne Manor? And with all the revolutions in technology, what would today's Batmobile be like?

All of this raced through the capacious mind of director Christopher Nolan as he took on the assignment of BATMAN BEGINS...a radically different kind of filmmaking experience than his previous projects. Chris gathered a small team: screenwriter David Goyer, producer Emma Thomas, production designer Nathan Crowley. An old garage began

to fill with concept art—images from comics, cityscapes, even a small, improbable Batmobile. More people joined the team, and the effort expanded from the garage to fill a film studio, in and above city streets, and location shoots across the world. Through it all, the images that had formed first in Chris' mind came to reality, frame by frame.

The result is a film that is both true to the essence of Batman as we have known him for decades, and a fresh and revealing look at Batman's character as we have never had the opportunity to see before. I had the pleasure of watching the film come to life from the offices at Warner Bros., DC Comics, that infamous garage, and even the lawn of Wayne Manor on a very rainy day, and it was watching magic of the highest order. I hope that the pages of this book will take you behind the scenes with me and let you enjoy that magic too. Close your eyes, hear the Batmobile's roar, and you'll start smelling the streets of Gotham as they burn...

Paul Levitz
President and Publisher
DC Comics

BEGINNINGS

ORIGIN

The character of Batman was originated by artist Bob Kane and writer Bill Finger. Asked to come up with a new super hero for DC Comics' *Detective Comics*, Kane first looked to Superman, who had debuted in 1938 in DC's *Action Comics*, as a starting point on which he could experiment. He tried adding wings to his character and this took his thoughts to the ornithopter, the flying machine designed by Leonardo da Vinci, essentially a glider with bat-like wings, which in turn led to his recalling one of his favorite films, *The Bat Whispers* from 1930 that featured a costumed killer known as the Bat. Further inspiration came from the 1920 film *The Mask of Zorro*, in which a wealthy fop transforms himself at night into a masked crusader fighting for justice. With Finger's help, Kane revised and improved his super hero's cowl, adding bat ears and changing the cumbersome wings to a cape.

While Kane had been working on creating a physical image for his new super hero, Finger needed to find inspiration as to how Batman's character and story would come to life through the comic book pages. He was ultimately influenced by D'Artagnan from Alexandre Dumas' 1844 novel *The Three Musketeers*, Sir Arthur Conan Doyle's detective Sherlock Holmes, and various contemporary pulp magazines.

The first Batman story appeared in *Detective Comics # 27* in May 1939, and from that moment, it was clear that DC Comics' new character was going to make a big impact.

In the spring of 1940 the character of Batman was deemed successful enough to warrant a dedicated comic, and by October 1943, Batman comic strips were syndicated in newspapers across the United States. As Bob Kane then noted, "That's the big time."

Indeed, throughout the 1940s Batman's popularity increased as movies and radio exposure helped to make him a household name. By the 1950s, however, Batman was being attacked on moral grounds, and with the rise of science fiction writing was overwhelmed with otherworldly visitors. During the mid-1960s the stories had become too far-fetched, and Batman had transmuted into so many different characters, from 'The Zebra Batman' and 'The Merman Batman' to 'Rip Van Batman,' that there was no heart left to the character, and in 1967 Bob Kane retired from active participation in the comics.

However, a new start for Batman came in 1986, when DC Comics decided that all of their hero characters had amassed too much complicated history and they decided to reintroduce them to the modern reader. In 1987, Frank Miller, who had already revolutionized the look of the comic with his *The Dark Knight Returns,* was assigned to script a four issue story arc entitled *Batman: Year One*.

INSPIRATIONS

Batman's origin story first appeared in *Detective Comics #33*; six months after the Batman series first began, as a two page story entitled "The Batman and How He Came to Be".

Writer/director Christopher Nolan and screenwriter David Goyer collaborated very closely on the script for BATMAN BEGINS. Nolan describes how they looked back over the entire body of work to see "what elements have stuck through that history. Those were then the key elements that we felt helped to pin down the character and the mythology that we had to stick to, and within that we felt free to interpret."

David Goyer sees Frank Miller's *Batman: Year One* as a definite starting point for the script. Frank Miller did not want to change the history of Batman, but rather preferred to make his mark by altering the tone of his work. Gotham City was shown as an incredibly corrupt setting against which honest citizens such as Bruce Wayne, Alfred, and the newly arrived policeman James Gordon stood out in stark contrast. Explains Goyer: "I think that *Batman: Year One* is one of the best Batman stories written. We were intrigued with the depiction of a young, untested Batman. I also enjoyed seeing how Gordon and Batman first met, and was interested in further mining that emerging relationship. In terms of other comic book influences, the work by Jeph Loeb and Tim Sale helped provide guidance."

Nolan cites *The Long Halloween,* and particularly *The Man Who Falls,* as other big inspirations on the film. The name of the character Ducard comes from the latter story, as does the idea of him traveling around the world: "I would say that *The Man Who Falls* is very, very important, leading into *Batman: Year One*, which makes up part of the middle act of our film, along with elements from *The Long Halloween*, [then] moving on to our own idea of where the story could lead."

BATMAN REINVENTED: THE SCRIPT

For Christopher Nolan, the key factor to making a Batman film was to ensure that there was a realistic element to the work and that Batman be presented as an extraordinary figure against the backdrop of a regular setting. "I felt that we had never before seen the specialness and otherworldly nature of the character against an ordinary world, so that the audiences would be as astounded by this character as the inhabitants of the cinematic world. That's the key to adopting a realist approach."

Wanting to base the script within the context of the comic books, he nonetheless did not want to make a comic book film. He explains: "We have tried to come up with the cinematic equivalent of the key elements of the comic book mythology, not literally aping the form of the comic book itself, so all the elements of design, photography, and the selection of storyline are based upon the same sort of terms of logic, realism, and attention to detail that would apply to any thriller or action film. This was important to me, because my experience of reading a comic is not one of being constantly aware of the form. In a really good comic you lose yourself, you fill in all the spaces between the panels, so we've created the cinematic equivalent of the experience of reading the comic – of putting the audience into the experience of Batman rather than standing outside it looking in on it in a two-dimensional way."

David Goyer gives details on specific changes from the comic books in terms of how characters have changed and evolved in the script to allow for their reinterpretation of the story. In particular, Lucius Fox "exists as a kind of ally for Bruce in the comics – but we pushed that relationship further and had him function as a kind of 'Q' character. Lucius is to Bruce as Q is to Bond. We've planted the notion that Lucius may very well suspect who Batman is."

One of the more major additions is the character of Rachel. "She is an invention of ours. We wanted a female lead who would be integral to the mystery/crime aspects of the story, but there didn't seem to be an appropriate character in the existing canon. In the Jeph Loeb/Tim Sale comics, Batman, Gordon and Harvey Dent form a kind of trinity. The three become allies. In effect, Rachel serves the same function as a pre-Two-Face Harvey Dent. Batman needed an ally in the D.A.'s office, but it's also convenient that that ally is someone Bruce had a history with. Being a childhood friend of Bruce's, Rachel also helps track the through line of Bruce's developments. She was there at the beginning, was there to witness Bruce as an angry young man, and is there when Bruce takes on the Batman mantle."

Finally, David Goyer notes, "Another notion that comes to mind is the idea that Batman may have inadvertently created a kind of arms race with respect to future super-villains. Chris and I were attracted to the idea that as Batman employs more extreme methods to fight crime, the villains would respond with similarly extreme methods and personalities."

GHOSTS FROM THE PAST

Director Christopher Nolan has created a very realistic interpretation of the Batman story, ensuring throughout that there was an explanation for every aspect of Batman's journey. "In BATMAN BEGINS we attempt to explain the purpose of the symbol to justify the approach of our character and why he wears the costume. We have given it a psychological reality in a realistic setting."

As the film starts, young Bruce Wayne and his friend Rachel Dawes are playing in the grounds of Wayne Manor when Bruce falls down a well and is besieged by bats. Overcome by fear, Bruce's phobia of bats deepens when he is taken to the opera by his parents and has to leave the theatre as the stage is overwhelmed by bats used as props in the opera. Exiting from a back door, the family is set upon by passing petty criminal Joe Chill, who demands money and jewelry

from Thomas and Martha Wayne before killing them in cold blood.

Nolan explains that by using the bat as his symbol "Bruce Wayne struggles to deal with his own fear. It felt like something original to us, the idea of taking his own weakness and making it his strength... I think it helps connect the strength that he would see in the symbol with the idea of portraying realistically why he would truly adopt the symbol in such an extreme and theatrical way. I think it's one of the most important elements of the film that we flesh out and develop in the character – an attempt to fuse and clarify certain elements of the mythology that have always been around. We try to crystallize the idea of a man who becomes his own fear in order to achieve power over others through that."

INT. GOTHAM OPERA HOUSE

A gilded house packed to the rafters for Boito's *Mefistofle*. Young Bruce
seated between his parents. On stage: WITCH-LIKE CREATURES cavort.
DARK BIRDS on wires descend, FLAPPING.

Young Bruce STARES, uneasy, at their VIOLENT motions.

INSERT CUT: BATS EXPLODE FROM A DARK CREVICE.

Young Bruce starts breathing faster, STARING fixedly.

SCREECHING, FLAPPING BLACK BATS SWARM ALL AROUND...

Young Bruce, gulping PANIC breaths, looks around for an exit- they're in
the middle of a row. He GRABS his dad's arm.

> YOUNG BRUCE
> (desperate whisper)
> Can we go?!

Young Bruce looks down at the bodies of his parents. DROPS to his
knees, head down; PEARLS dot the asphalt beneath him. Some of
them are bloody.

YOUNG BRUCE
I miss them, Alfred.
I miss them so much.

ALFRED
(whispering)
So do I, Master Bruce.
So do I.

ALFRED

"**Everybody** has a picture of who Alfred is, and I think we've rounded that picture out rather more, in that in our film, he's not just a butler and the man who can make things happen, he's a real father figure to Bruce and there's an emotional link between them." (Emma Thomas, Producer)

Growing up in Wayne Manor, just the two of them, Alfred is the closest thing that Bruce has to a father, and their relationship demonstrates this - their conversations reveal a closeness, an intimate knowledge of one another, and an enormous trust. Alfred also knows that he can make Bruce aware if he feels he's doing something wrong, while always remembering that he is also the butler.

Explains Christopher Nolan: "Alfred represents the emotional center of the film, and Michael Caine is a great scene stealer, and I encouraged him to do that as much as possible because I feel that Alfred as a character is a scene stealer – he has a wonderfully dry wit in the comics that Michael was able to get across on the screen, and there's a great warmth and humor to the portrayal which plays very nicely against Bruce Wayne."

Michael Caine sees Alfred very much as Bruce Wayne's guide and mentor, offering practical help where necessary: "Alfred is a tremendous help in that way, but basically he sets the mind of the boy to make the man...he's the one constant in his life...and his moral conscience, too".

Adds Christian Bale, "It's a great relationship. I find it a very funny one, as well as very touching." Alfred tries to keep Bruce safe and is happy to criticize where necessary, but also provides some genuine comic relief to the story.

BRUCE WAYNE:
WARRIOR

OLD MAN
They are going to fight you.

WAYNE
Again?

OLD MAN
Until they kill you.

ENORMOUS MAN

(broken English)

You are in hell, little man...

DUCARD

The world is too small for someone like Bruce
Wayne to disappear...
(gestures around them)
No matter how deep he chooses to sink.

WAYNE

Who are you?

DUCARD

My name is merely Ducard. But I speak for
Rā's al Ghūl. A man greatly feared by the
criminal underworld. A man who can offer
you a path.

WAYNE

What makes you think I need a path?

Ducard looks around the cell.

Someone like you is only here by choice. You've
been exploring the criminal fraternity... But
whatever your original intentions... You've
become truly *lost*.

Wayne struggles through DRIVING SNOW up an ICY RIDGE...

He clears the ridge, FLOPS down into the snow. Painfully raises his scarf-wrapped face to the cutting wind to see a MONASTERY perched on jagged rock.

INT. GREAT HALL, MONASTERY

Wayne shuffles forward into a low-ceilinged wooden
hall lit by flickering lamps. Hands trembling, Wayne
pulls at brittle scarves. He STARTS as the doors
THUD shut behind him.

THE ENIGMATIC DUCARD

"Ducard's name is drawn from a character in *The Man Who Falls* whom Bruce encounters on his travels, and we have used that as a jumping off point to create a character who is Bruce's mentor, the influence on his life that guides him down a particular path and initiates him into worlds of skill, philosophy, and so forth. We thought the idea interesting, of Bruce searching round the world, not knowing really what he's looking for, and then being found by this character, who has answers to his questions."

Bruce Wayne has been thrown into solitary confinement in a Bhutanese jail following a vicious fight with some of the other inmates. Filthy, exhausted, and suffering from an inability to channel his rage, Ducard catches him at a vulnerable moment. Entering his cell, he offers Bruce salvation. Explains actor Liam Neeson, who plays Ducard: "Ducard seems to suddenly appear to offer him a path out of his torture. The path requires rigorous training; incredible discipline of mind and body, and having attained that he can hopefully take on evil in the world...a path with a destiny."

Following a quest set by his new mentor, Bruce seeks him out in a monastery high in the Himalayas where he undergoes exhaustive training. Ducard is a disciplinarian whose quest is to serve his master, Rā's al Ghūl in finding a natural justice in the world. Aided by the League of Shadows, a brotherhood of highly skilled mercenary ninja fighters, they are committed to doing whatever is necessary to rid the world of all evil.

Liam Neeson understood Ducard's philosophy, which reflects Rā's al Ghūl's teachings as this: "you have to go into yourself to discover the dark side of yourself as well as the good side, and to be able to marry these forces in order to be able to achieve your full potential as a human being."

An undeniably inscrutable character, Ducard sets himself up as a father figure to Bruce, though Neeson admits that "everything is not as it seems."

DUCARD

What are you seeking?

WAYNE

I... I seek... the means to fight injustice. To turn fear against
those who prey on the fearful...

Rā's al Ghūl speaks.

DUCARD (translating)

To manipulate the fears of others you must first master your own.
(his own words)
Are you ready to begin?

R Ā ' S A L G H Ū L

The character of Rā's al Ghūl was created by Dennis O'Neil and first appeared in the Batman comics in the 1970s. He has always been presented as an immortal and mysterious figure whose aim was world domination.

Explains screenwriter David Goyer: "Denny created Rā's al Ghūl, in part, I think, as reaction to the James Bond films that were so popular at the time. Rā's is the most 'Bond-like' of Batman's rogues. His scope is broader than the Joker's or the Riddler's. He's not simply concerned with Gotham, but the world as a whole. Denny was one of the first writers to take Bruce Wayne out of Gotham, which we also felt added to the scope of the story. In Denny's stories, Rā's also somewhat functioned as a father figure, and this gave us the opportunity to tweak that relationship a bit more and turn Rā's into a fully-fledged mentor."

His presence is impenetrable in BATMAN BEGINS. Bruce Wayne first encounters this shadowy figure in the Himalayan monastery, where Ducard is training him in Rā's al Ghūl's physical and philosophical teachings.

Rā's al Ghūl is a complex, illusory character, seemingly calm and quiet, but described by Ken Watanabe, who plays him in the film, as "a silent volcano."

BRUCE'S TRAINING BEGINS

Bruce Wayne has grown up in a decaying Gotham City that has become increasingly hostile since the death of his father and is now run by morally corrupt officials. Disillusioned with what he sees and unable to see how he can possibly reverse the damage, he sets off on a journey for a number of years, putting himself in dangerous and destructive places in an attempt to gain some kind of knowledge that will help him fight injustice.

Bruce Wayne's first on-screen fight is in the Bhutanese jail. Picked on by a number of inmates, Bruce defends himself through bravery and some skill, but essentially the fight is more about courage and brutality. He has an inner anger that overwhelms him, and the audience sees him at his most raw.

After journeying to the Himalayan monastery, he is trained and mentored by the mysterious Ducard and made to fight with the League of Shadows. From them he learns not only how to sharpen his reflexes, but how to detect a person's energy even if they are covered in body armor. Bruce is also tutored in effective swordfighting, taking on Ducard on a frozen, cracking ice lake and in his ultimate initiation, fights Rā's al Ghūl.

Christopher Nolan wanted to keep the fighting style as realistic as possible, but at the same time wanted something different, that an audience would not instantly recognize, a fighting style that was both brutal yet real. He explains: "There are a lot of martial arts in the film, but we did not want to make a martial arts film with a lot of dancelike kung fu moves. There's a lot of skill and knowledge about different martial arts, but we wanted a realistic underpinning to the fist fight – the most effective form of violence being a combination of a number of different skills; controlled fear and aggression being primary factors. We wanted the fights to have quite a gritty edge to them and not be too fanciful."

Dave Foreman, the film's fight coordinator, started Christian Bale training in a number of martial arts styles until it was suggested that a new martial art, never before seen on the big screen, called the Keysi Fighting Method, might be appropriate. Based on twenty years of extensive research, Keysi has been developed by Andy Norman and Justo Dieguez, who taught the actors a pared down version of their fighting style, based more on philosophy and balance than physical combat. Explains Bale: "It's this very intuitive kind of martial art, but also very brutal. It's all about going for the break straightaway!"

Through the fights, Wayne's mental and physical journey is explored. From a streetwise kid who doesn't mind getting beaten up, over the course of BATMAN BEGINS he develops his fighting skills to become Batman.

DUCARD
Your anger gives you great power, but if
you let it, it will destroy you.

DUCARD

Theatricality and deception are powerful agents. You must become *more* than just a man in the mind of your opponent.

DUCARD

To conquer fear, you must *become* fear... you must bask in the
fear of other men... and men fear most what they cannot *see-*

MERE FEET FROM THE CLIFF EDGE, Wayne GRABS Ducard- raises his free GAUNTLET-CLAD ARM, and SMASHES AT THE ICE, DIGGING IN with BRONZE SCALLOPS... STOPPING on the edge- Ducard HANGS LIMPLY over a tremendous drop- Wayne STRUGGLES with the dead weight. Wayne PULLS Ducard up onto the ice.

INT. PRIVATE JET - DAWN

Wayne sits, drink in hand, ragged against rich leather.

> ALFRED
> Are you coming back to Gotham for long, sir?

> WAYNE
> As long as it takes.

Alfred looks at Wayne, curious.

> WAYNE (CONT'D)
> I'm going to show the people of Gotham that
> the city doesn't belong to the criminals and
> the corrupt.
>
> People need dramatic examples to shake them
> out of apathy. I can't do this as Bruce Wayne.
> A man is just flesh-and-blood, and can be
> ignored or destroyed. But a symbol... as a
> symbol I can be incorruptible, everlasting...

> ALFRED
> What symbol?

> WAYNE
> I'm not sure yet. Something elemental.
> Something terrifying.

THE BATMAN
APPEARS

3

INT. GREENHOUSE

Now derelict. Glass cracked or missing, paint peeled from wrought iron.
Wayne stands in the entrance, remembering-

INT. CAVERNS

Wayne climbs down a jagged rock crevice. Air blows in his face. The crevice WIDENS into a low-ceilinged chamber. Wayne hears the RUSH of WATER. He crouches, advances through the low chamber. It turns DOWNWARDS, steeper- Wayne carefully slides on his back, LOWERING HIMSELF into...

LIMITLESS BLACK. Wayne stands. A ROAR of water now. He REACHES into his coat, pulls out a CHEMICAL TORCH. CRACKS it, throwing LIGHT into...

A VAST CAVERN. An underground RIVER, a JAGGED ceiling, far above, which as Wayne PEERS, starts to *MOVE* —

BATS EXPLODE from the ceiling. THOUSANDS DESCEND, SCREECHING, attracted to the
light- Wayne instinctively CROUCHES. But as they SWARM around him terrifyingly...

Wayne RISES to his feet amidst a CYCLONE of bats, watching the fluttering blackness with
profound CALM.

And he knows the symbol he must use.

INT. EARLE'S OFFICE, WAYNE ENTERPRISES

WAYNE
I'm not here to interfere-
I'm looking for a job.
(off look)
I just want to get to know the
company that my family built.

EARLE
Any idea where you'd start?

WAYNE
Applied Sciences caught my eye.

EARLE
(surprised)
Mr. Fox's department?
(shrugs)
Perfect. I'll make a call.

Wayne Industries was developed as a philanthropic company by Thomas Wayne and was left to his son on his death. Always striving to do good works for Gotham City, and with a vision for the future, Thomas Wayne commissioned and built among other things, the city's monorail.

In Bruce's absence, and under the leadership of William Earle, Wayne Industries has turned into a company based more on the self interest of its directors than the good works of Thomas Wayne. Lucius Fox, an old friend of Thomas Wayne, has been sidelined to the department of Applied Sciences, where Earle feels he can do no harm. The Applied Sciences division is, however, a gold mine of cutting edge technological products and prototypes that Bruce soon adapts for his own purposes.

Christopher Nolan sees Lucius Fox as an important ally for Bruce Wayne: "The film presents various surrogate father figures, and I would count Lucius as one of those. He is an important mentor figure to Bruce back in Gotham, and we felt that this was emotionally important as well as for the mechanical reason that Bruce should have a conduit into Wayne Enterprises that would allow him through the back door to utilize his own great wealth from the corporation founded by his father."

Lucius does not really believe that Bruce's interest in the gadgets he has helped develop is purely for the purposes of spelunking (cave exploring), Bruce's new hobby, but he goes along with it, out of loyalty to Thomas Wayne. As Morgan Freeman, who plays Lucius Fox, explains: "A bond starts to develop between them, because I think Lucius sees that the young Wayne is now ready to pick up the reigns of the company and put it back on its feet where it should be, and he also has an inkling as to who this young man is becoming."

It is in the Applied Sciences Division that Bruce is introduced to a number of prototypes that will come to make up the tools of his trade.

FOX

Guess they never thought about marketing to the billionare base-jumping, spelunking market.

WAYNE

Look, Mr. Fox, if you're uncomfortable —

FOX

Mr. Wayne, if you don't tell me what you're really doing, then when I get asked... I don't have to lie. But don't treat me like an idiot.

Wayne GRINDS METAL at a lathe. Alfred approaches with a thermos.
Wayne stops grinding, BLOWS on his handiwork... Alfred looks at the
steel carved into a BAT'S WING.

    ALFRED
    Why the *bat*, Master Wayne?

    WAYNE
    Bats frighten me.
    (slight smile)
    And it's time my enemies shared my dread.

BECOMING THE BATMAN

"**You can't really** play Batman until you're in the Batsuit... he's got to be somebody who's intimidating to tough guys who are used to coming up against tough guys." Christian Bale

Lindy Hemming, costume designer on BATMAN BEGINS, approached the design of the Batsuit from a position of realism, basing it on the practical manner in which Bruce Wayne comes upon the various elements that make up his Batman costume. The suit started off as a combat outfit designed in Lucius Fox's laboratory as a survival suit. Hemming wanted the prototype to be see-through, in order that "you'd be able to see the part inside which protects the body, that helps you survive... the combat suit's made of waterproof armor, with components inside that maintain body temperature and keep the muscles from freezing up. It's multifunctional...and Bruce goes into his workshop and starts to tinker with it, and you see how he develops it from that into the black Batsuit."

Christopher Nolan was very involved in the design of the Batsuit: "We've attempted to portray the costume that emerges from a reading of the history of the character and an analysis of all the artwork that has been done over the years on the character."

Making the Batsuit and its accessories required a huge team of people, who set themselves up in a number of workshops behind Shepperton Studios just outside London codenamed "Capetown." Nolan had a number of requests regarding the design of the Batsuit, including that it be supple enough that Batman could turn his head and fight unencumbered, and that it should be entirely matte, thus enabling Batman to lurk in the shadows.

The Batsuit itself comprises a neoprene undersuit (like a wet suit for diving) with molded cream latex sections stuck onto it, and over 1,000kg of latex was used to make approximately 40 Batsuits. The process started with Christian Bale having a life cast made, leading to clay sculptures out of which molds were made. These were then injected with a foam mixture, cooked in a commercial baking oven, and then the pieces were trimmed and glued onto the undersuit. As a result, the Batsuit has no seams.

The cape also incorporates elements taken from the Applied Sciences Division. It was essential to the creative team that the cape be supple, yet, as the story dictates, go rigid so that Batman could glide. Thanks to Lucius Fox's invention of a fabric that when hit with an electrical impulse would stiffen, this was achieved.

In fact, the costume design team itself could have worked in Applied Sciences. They invented the very fabric used in reality for the cape from a waterproof nylon parachute silk which was then electrostatically flocked (the fabric is glued, and then a static electric charge is put through the material, after which a fine dust is dropped onto the material which clings to it) to create a velvety feel.

Christopher Nolan was very specific to all of his team as to the way Batman was to move around in the film. He wanted it to be as realistic as possible, as Batman has no superpowers to help him. It was essential, therefore, that there be a credible way that the cape could help Batman to fly. With the help of the special effects team, Batman could trigger his cape to go rigid, and with a lot of help from a wire winch was effectively able to glide. Almost all of the flying scenes in the film were shot as live-action. Explains Nolan:

"Probably the biggest difference of our costume from previous film and television interpretations is the use of the cape as it appears in the comics, which is very dramatic. Long and flowing and matte black, it is used to conceal and for attack, and the cape plays a large part in our film. When we're portrayingBatman visually, we try to use the cape in the way the comics have used it, particularly the more recent comics, which with very fine artwork incorporates the drama of the cape."

Finally, the cowl completes Bruce Wayne's costume. Hemming was pleased with the design of this, and a lot of time was spent sculpting, discussing, and refining this iconic mask: "I love the sensitiveness of it, the fact that you can feel the workings of his face underneath it. Although it is solid around his temples and face, you feel it is still able to move like a face." Adds Nolan: "I was looking for something that had some of the aggression that the character has in the comics... but also a more organic look to the facial elements of the cowl. We didn't want it to look machinelike, so we took it back to its roots."

FALCONE'S EMPIRE

Says Christopher Nolan: "Corruption is rife in Gotham, and it's very, very important to the story, because the only world in which somebody of Bruce Wayne's position can be inspired to become Batman is a world in which the conventional means of fighting justice are denied, and corruption for David Goyer and me was key to that. In a society that is corrupt and where the institutions of the law are not respected by the criminals and do not have the power they are supposed to have, that starts to explain why Bruce Wayne could not become a crusading district attorney or judge, or run for office, or join the police – those institutions have become too corrupt."

Carmine Falcone is the head of organized crime in Gotham City, and is played by actor Tom Wilkinson, who describes him as "an all round bad egg – nothing loveable about him." He is the last villain that Bruce Wayne confronts prior to leaving Gotham City on his travels and the first that he tackles as Batman when he returns.

For Christopher Nolan, the character presents an immense force: "Falcone represents the extreme corruption in Gotham because he's a powerful organized crime figure, who clearly feels no threat from the law or forces of justice in Gotham City, and he therefore personifies the need for another force to restore law and order – only Batman can touch him."

Jumpy Thug FIRES blindly at STROBING SHADOWS- GLIMPSES of
a DARK, CLOAKED FIGURE moving from SHADOW TO SHADOW.
Jumpy Thug empties the clip. FUMBLES for another...

     JUMPY THUG
     WHERE ARE YOU?!!!

A whispered word at his ear:

     BATMAN
     Here.

BAMAN'S FACE, UPSIDE DOWN, at the Thug's shoulder- Jumpy
Thug SCREAMS as he is ENFOLDED by DARKNESS —

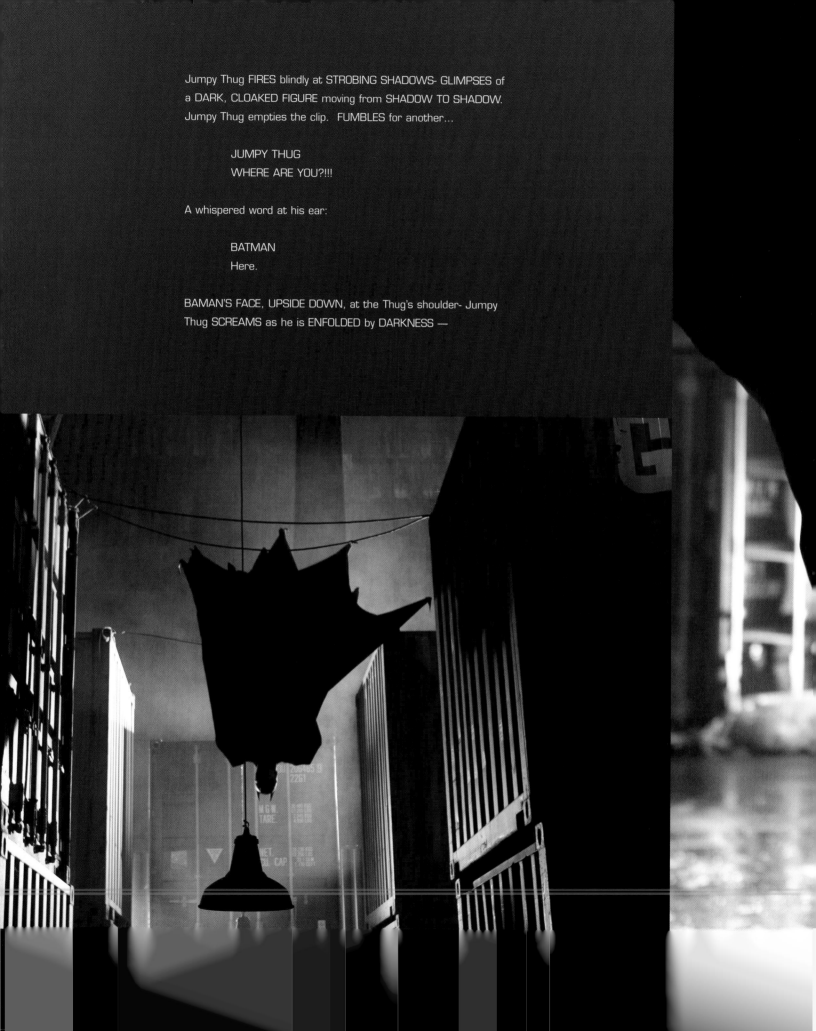

Falcone is STRAPPED to the LIGHT, UNCONSCIOUS, arms spread.
Coat RIPPED, hanging from his arms in a STRANGE PATTERN.

          COP 1
          The hell *is* that? Looks like...

Gordon follows their gaze up to where the BEAM of light CASTS
FALCONE'S SHADOW onto the CLOUDS.

          COP 2
          Like a *bat*.

GOTHAM CITY

Bill Finger, the original writer of the Batman comic, settled on the name Gotham City in 1941 after the comic had been going for some two years. It had previously been acknowledged that New York was the setting of Batman, but Finger did not want anybody to identify Gotham City with any existing place.

By the start of BATMAN BEGINS, Gotham City has become a dark, bleak, and decaying place, very far from the city that Thomas Wayne had tried to improve with his philanthropic works. The city's officials, to the highest degree, are greedy and corrupt and have no interest in civic duty, and the city has fallen to ruin as slums have built up among the garbage.

Production designer Nathan Crowley set about creating his own very specific landscape for Gotham City. New York, Tokyo, and Chicago (where some filming took place) were all inspirations, and the slum area of the city which was known as the Narrows was based on the shanty town of Kowloon in Hong Kong, which was demolished in 1994. Geographically, like New York, Gotham City comprises several islands, with the Narrows and Arkham Asylum on a smaller island, reminiscent of Roosevelt Island, and Wayne Manor, under which the Batcave is located, is set up on the Palisades above New York, where rock formations could credibly create an enormous cave.

Explains Crowley, "We wanted this film to be as realistic as possible to a city that might exist, so audiences really feel that this place *could* exist. It's not a fantasy, it's something familiar." Gotham City has been made up of sets, locations, and some miniatures, but, as Crowley continues, "they're all from existing architecture; we start with something real and then enhance it, because you can't beat real life, nothing looks as good. We wanted to reinvent Gotham... and the realism was our reinvention."

But the physical location of Gotham City is only part of the importance of the city within the context of Batman's world. Explains David Goyer: "In the comic books it's always been established that the Waynes had a long history with Gotham – that their destinies were intertwined. We wanted to convey that in our film. We wanted Bruce's father to instill his son with a certain sense of stewardship. It's another reason why Bruce chooses to become Batman – because he simply can't abandon the city that his forefathers helped build."

He continues: "In our film, as in the comics, Gotham is very corrupt – rotten to the core. But we didn't want it to always have been that way. Originally, the city was a much more hopeful place. We wanted the city to fall on hard times after Bruce's father dies. We were trying to establish that Thomas Wayne was basically the king/patriarch of Gotham. After his death, while Bruce was coming of age, the city basically fell to the savages. Our film takes place as Bruce is just returning to the kingdom, fighting to reclaim it."

RACHEL

Daughter to the housekeeper at Wayne Manor, Rachel Dawes is one of Bruce Wayne's oldest friends and is a character that has been invented for the film by Nolan and Goyer. Explains Nolan: "We felt right from the beginning that we needed to introduce a childhood friend of Bruce's as a character who starts very close to him, but from whom he has to isolate himself as time passes, an isolation that is compounded when he becomes Batman."

Rachel and Bruce have been playmates since childhood. Indeed, it is when they are playing together on the grounds of Wayne Manor that Bruce falls down the well and is engulfed by bats – an event that will change him forever.

They are out of touch while Bruce is travelling, and the first time that they see one another as adults is disappointing for Rachel. By then an Assistant District Attorney, she sees Bruce surrounded by models and displaying the trappings of his wealth. Rachel has had to work very hard to reach the position where she feels she may be able to do some good in Gotham City and wants Bruce to step up to his responsibilities as well. Explains actress Katie Holmes, who plays Rachel: "She has a line in the movie where she says it's not who you are underneath but what you do that defines you. And I think that speaks volumes about how idealistic she is. She's really this type of person that wants to do good in the world. She wants to save her city and to help people... I feel like that line says so much about her and about their relationship...and how much she wants him to see what's right and to use what he was given to do good in the world."

Rachel's first encounter with Batman is at the monorail train station. On her way home from work she is being chased by a thug, and Batman swoops down to save her and give her some incriminating photographs of a corrupt judge.

Producer Emma Thomas is very keen on the addition of Rachel as a character in the film. "What I love about Rachel is that she provides the parallel to Bruce's journey. They are both terrifically disillusioned by the way things are working in Gotham and they know that things need to change, so they're both the same in that regard, but they choose different paths in their quest to change things. Rachel thinks she can do this from within the system, so she's working in the District Attorney's office and she's trying to fix the rules, but Bruce decides he has to step outside of the law to change things. I like watching their parallel journeys... they're both as passionate about the end result as each other, they are just taking different paths."

The Applied Sciences Division

at Wayne Industries offers Bruce Wayne state of the art prototypes that he can modify to suit his own specific purposes.

The Batmobile started off as a military vehicle called the Tumbler, created to jump over ditches and pull bridges out. It was the first thing that director Christopher Nolan asked production designer Nathan Crowley to design when the BATMAN BEGINS screenplay was still being written. The car was going to take some time to build, so an art department was set up in Nolan's garage and they started making models out of anything they could find, ending up ultimately with a cross between a Lamborghini and a Hummer.

From the final design, eight Batmobiles were made at three workshops at Shepperton Studios – built entirely from scratch and not customized or remodelled from any existing cars. One of Nolan's requests was that he wanted the front wheels to be held from the side with no front axel on the car. Initially sceptical, workshop supervisor Andy Smith and special effects coordinator Chris Corbould were eventually able to find a way to make the design a reality. The Batmobile has six wheels, weighs two and a half tons, has jumped a distance of sixty feet, and has driven at speeds of over 100 miles per hour. Indeed, the Batmobile could perform at such high speeds that during chase scenes, it was sometimes hard for a tracking helicopter to keep up. The Batmobile has been so well-realized that it can truly achieve all the stunts that the story required. Barely necessitating a need for CGI enhancement, the vehicle performed almost everything the audience sees on the screen. Adds Chris Nolan: "The Batmobile design stage was enormously exciting. The fact that Chris and Andy could then build it for real so we could drive this thing that we'd built out of plastic model kits and it could do all the things that the script ever asked it to do was amazing – it becomes a character in the film."

Bruce Wayne also picked up a number of other gadgets from the Applied Sciences Division which he adapted to suit his particular needs.

Batman's utility belt was modified from a climbing harness. The first time that Batman appears in his prototype suit to Sergeant Gordon he wears the entire harness. With time, however, Bruce removes the chest straps and leaves just the belt with its magnetic strips to ensure that the tools of his trade are instantly available to him. Christopher Nolan is particularly drawn to the utility belt: "It was beautifully made with those detachable magnetic pockets using earth magnets and an anodized metal finish – it was the real thing. It was exciting to play with that, the sound of it and the feel of it was something we tried to get on film. It was a really extraordinary piece of engineering."

Attached to the utility belt are a grappling gun which shoots a 350 lb test mono filament with a

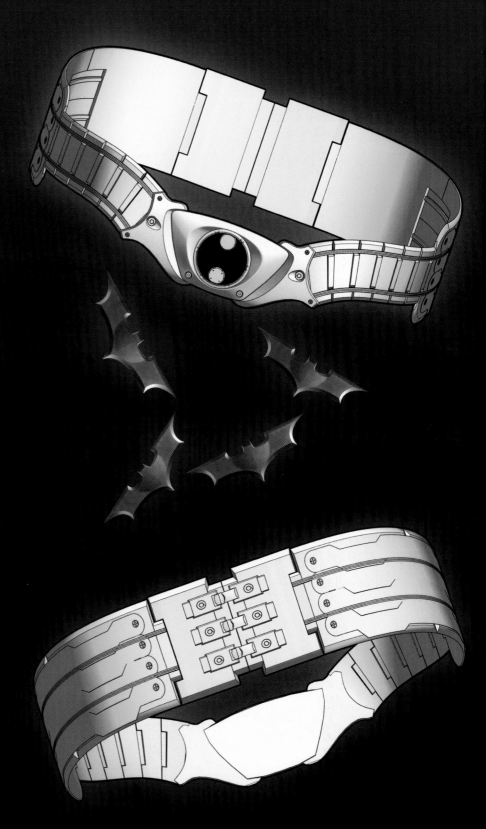

hook on the end which helps Batman to escape difficult situations, mini mines that help to create a distraction when needed, and Bruce, in his own workshop, also manufactures his ubiquitous Batarangs - sharp metal "bats" that fly like boomerangs.

As with all other areas of the film, these gadgets are set in a realistic foundation. The viewer is made aware that everything Batman uses has been invented and is possible to achieve, but due to its expense has never been manufactured. With money behind him, therefore, Batman has access to all kinds of superior gadgetry.

thought. When he heard that Christopher Nolan was going to direct BATMAN BEGINS, he knew that his Batman would be something entirely fresh. "It sounded like there were themes from the comic books I'd seen by creators like Jeph Loeb, Tim Sale and Frank Miller. It had that kind of a look and feel to it, which really intrigued me."

Bale certainly wanted his interpretation of the character to be something different to any other on-screen Batman, and to bring out the dichotomy of the unhealthy state of his mind, of his need for vengeance, balanced against a desire to make his philanthropic father proud of him. "This is a man who's been held in limbo all of his life because of his need to make right on the wrongs that were dealt out to his parents. So he has this contradiction and combat within himself. I always felt that the Batman persona was the means by which he was able to live something of a normal life as Bruce Wayne."

One of the reasons that Batman has endured for so long in the public conscience is that he has constantly reinvented himself over the years. In BATMAN BEGINS, Bale and Nolan broke down the Bruce Wayne/Batman character into a number of parts. As Bruce Wayne there was the playboy – a spoiled, wealthy womanizer that he could use to camou-flage his other nocturnal life; Bruce Wayne the genuine man – whom he would reveal to only those he could trust, such as Alfred and Rachel; vengeful Bruce Wayne – who has hate within him and no interest in his future; and also young Bruce Wayne – who witnessed the murder of his parents, and the unfocused college Bruce Wayne before he goes on his

Bale ensures that his Batman has certain ethical rules by which he abides, always aware of why Bruce Wayne has this alter ego, and that Bruce must never start to enjoy his nocturnal persona. "That's something I like to play with, with him as Batman - that he can very easily start to enjoy it. And that's a very fine line between him and the villains, and he must maintain a higher moral code."

He continues: "Personally what I like and what Chris [Nolan] likes is fantasy that you can imagine being genuinely grounded in reality." Batman has no superpowers, he is a rich man who has learned skills and who puts himself physically at risk in order to do the job he feels he must. The suspense of the character comes from him being a real man - if he's infallible there is no suspense.

Christopher Nolan knew that finding the right person to play this extraordinary range in one character would be essential. He explains: "When it came to casting, our biggest hurdle was to find someone who could play a character who's capable of and determined to transform from Bruce Wayne to Batman. You are therefore looking for somebody who exhibits incredible confidence and skill in their physical prowess, but also an extraordinary level of dedication and focus, so you can look at their eyes and believe that this person could choose to make this transformation and would succeed in doing so. Christian has that incredible level of determination and intensity that you really believe he can do these things – he really became the character."

"Gordon represents the good that is still in Gotham and is essentially dormant, either in other peoples' cases through apathy, or in Gordon's case through isolation. There is only so much he can do as one man except live right. It's not that Gotham is an inherently evil place; it's just that it has become corrupt, and that starts to explain what Bruce realistically hopes to achieve as Batman. He wants to tip the scales in Gotham back toward good, through example, and through fighting the worst of the offenders and showing the good people of Gotham that they can stand up for themselves and reclaim their city." (Christopher Nolan)

The origin story set out in BATMAN BEGINS also shows the long connection between Batman and Gordon, dating back to Bruce's childhood when they meet following the murders of Thomas and Martha Wayne.

Gordon is one of the only truly honest officials left in Gotham City, a man desperately clutching on to his integrity while all around him corruption is rife. The arrival of Batman provides a welcome relief, as Gary Oldman, who plays Gordon, explains: "There's a world-weariness to Gordon that Chris [Nolan] wanted. And he's infused with a new energy and hope with the emergence of Batman on the scene."

It is with Gordon that the audience first sees the prototype Batman that Bruce Wayne has created. Not yet a fully formed and costumed character, and wearing a balaclava in place of the soon to be finished cowl, Bruce as Batman nonetheless has an effect on Oldman's Gordon: "He's lurking in the shadows and he confronts me in the office. At first, I think maybe it's a one-off and he's just a bit of a nut. But obviously I get the sense that he means what he says, that there's a sincerity there…I can possibly trust this guy. He's a bit of a wild card, but his heart's in the right place and it's nice to have an ally."

Jim Gordon and Batman may approach the fight against evil in very different ways, but it is clear from the outset that they are both on the same side.

"Across the Batman's horizon moves a new and terrible figure – a fantastic figure of burlap and straw, with a brain cunning and distorted! Who is this figure whose very ludicrous appearance inspires fear... symbolizes fear... fear incarnate...fear walking the streets of Gotham City? It is that most terrible, most bizarre of all criminals...the criminal all will learn to fear and call...the Scarecrow!!" Introduced thus in *World's Finest Comics #3* in 1941, the Scarecrow's alter ego of Dr. Jonathan Crane only lasted for one more story, but would resurface many decades later to continue his reign of terror.

In BATMAN BEGINS, Dr. Jonathan Crane is a psychologist at Arkham Asylum, who, in cahoots with Rā's al Ghūl, is experimenting on a fear toxin which he tests on the inmates of the Asylum. Cillian Murphy, who embodies the dual role, enjoyed the appeal of playing a bad guy. "When you get to play an evil person, as an actor that's a bit of a thrill."

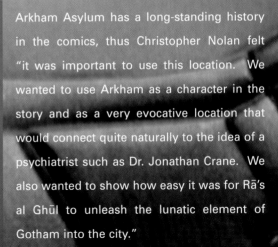

Drawing inspiration from the comics, Murphy feels that Crane would probably have been bullied as a kid and would have been quite reclusive: "He's not physically imposing but he has intelligence and this fear toxin that he's working on. What that does is bring everyone's worst fears to fruition...it's like your worst nightmare. It's deeply rooted in getting his own power back, I think – to see people reduced to sniveling wrecks, which I'm sure he had been as a child."

Lindy Hemming, the film's costume designer, continued the theme of Crane's physical imperfection by adjusting the size of his costumes to give him odd dimensions: "We made his body small and slim and tight and his jacket sleeves a bit too long... and the button we made in his jacket in the wrong place. We altered the balance of his body, just trying to make him not a perfect shape."

In keeping with the rest of the film, the Scarecrow's mask is also grounded in a sense of reality, as he can store his breathing apparatus under the burlap in order that he not inhale the fear toxin himself. Its more sinister effect is the horrific image it conjures to those who have breathed the toxin as they go insane from fear.

Arkham Asylum has a long-standing history in the comics, thus Christopher Nolan felt "it was important to use this location. We wanted to use Arkham as a character in the story and as a very evocative location that would connect quite naturally to the idea of a psychiatrist such as Dr. Jonathan Crane. We also wanted to show how easy it was for Rā's al Ghūl to unleash the lunatic element of Gotham into the city."

David Goyer is also interested in interpreting Arkham Asylum as a reflection of the film's narrative. "I've always felt that Arkham functioned as a real-world analogue for Bruce's own fractured personality. In a sense, it's a three dimensional abstraction. The model for Arkham was Bedlam, the London hospital that was originally established in the thirteenth century. A lot of people don't realize that the word (used today to mean chaos) was actually a real place. By the fourteenth century, Bedlam became a place to house the insane and has since become synonymous with asylums in general."

Crane reaches into his briefcase. Inside is a BREATHING APPARATUS
attached to a small BURLAP SACK MASK.

        CRANE
        Would you like to see my mask?

He pulls the mask out of the case. Holds it up.

        CRANE (CONT'D)
        I use it in my experiments. Probably not very frightening to a
        guy like you. But those crazies...

Falcone stares at Crane, uneasy. Crane puts on the mask. It is a sack
with eye holes and twine stitching for a mouth.

        CRANE (CONT'D)
        ...they can't stand it...

EXT. HOUSING PROJECT, THE NARROWS

Batman climbs silently along the wall, window to window. He stops at one, pulls a small black OPTIC from his utility belt, extends it into a tiny periscope. Angles it to look in the window: in the darkened apartment, the furniture is stacked up around the walls. In the center is a large pile of STUFFED RABBITS.

Batman turns to Crane- now wearing his MASK. Crane's hand FLASHES toward Batman, who
DODGES a small puff of SMOKE. Batman moves for Crane- COUGHS, CHOKES- losing BALANCE-
GASPING... Batman looks at Crane, sees a monster.

Batman REELS, in the throes of a hallucination. Crane SMASHES the BOTTLE over him, soaking
him with GASOLINE... Batman LURCHES for the windows, IMAGES ASSAULTING his mind.

Batman TURNS to Crane. Who holds a FLAMING LIGHTER.

     CRANE
     Need a light?

Crane TOSSES the lighter at Batman... who BURSTS into FLAMES.

INT. CORRIDOR, ARKHAM ASYLUM

Crane hurries along the corridor, heading for Rachel.

> CRANE
>
> Ms. Dawes, this is most irregular. I've nothing
> to add to the report I filed with the judge.

> RACHEL
>
> Well, I have questions about your report.
> (off look)
> Such as, isn't it convenient for a 52-year-old
> man with no history of mental illness to have a
> complete psychotic break just when he's about
> to be indicted?

> CRANE
>
> (motions)
> You can see for yourself, there's nothing
> convenient about his symptoms.

Rachel considers Falcone's terrified gaze.

> RACHEL
>
> What's "scarecrow?"

> CRANE
>
> Patients suffering delusional episodes often
> focus their paranoia onto an external tormentor,
> usually one conforming to Jungian archetypes.
> (shrugs)
> In this case, a scarecrow.

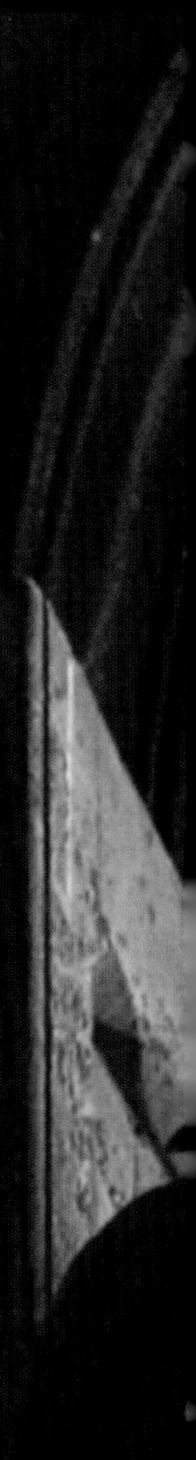

CRANE

Let me help you...

A small puff of GAS sprays from his sleeve. Rachel

RECOLS, coughing, choking.

CRANE
(fascinated)
He's here.

FIRST THUG
Who?

CRANE
The batman.

BATMAN
Taste of your own medicine, doctor?

GORDON
What's happened to her?

BATMAN
Crane poisoned her with a psychotropic hallucinogen.
(off look)
A panic-inducing toxin.

GORDON
Let me take her down to the medics-

BATMAN
They can't help her. But I can.

The BATMOBILE comes flying out of the darkness... the matte-black muscularity of the stealth-finished "car" BLOWS by.

The Batmobile SMASHES into the cop car, huge front
tires CRUSHING the bonnet, BOUNCING the Batmobile
right over the cop car in a messy display of brute force.

The Batmobile ROCKETS off the edge of the lookout, over the gorge, FLYING STRAIGHT AT THE FACE OF A WATERFALL.

RĀ'S AL GHŪL
You have no illusions about the world,
Bruce. When I found you in that jail you
were lost. But I believed in you. I took
away your fear and showed you a path.
You were my greatest student... it should
be *you* standing at my side, saving the
world.

WAYNE
I'll be standing right where I am now —
between you and the people of Gotham.

RĀ'S AL GHŪL

Tomorrow the world will watch in horror as its greatest city destroys
itself. The movement back to harmony will be unstoppable this time.

RĀ'S AL GHŪL
Time to spread the word...
and the word is...

Rā's al Ghūl rests his hand on the
machine's switch...

RĀ'S AL GHŪL
Panic.

CRANE

It's too late... you can't stop it.

Rachel turns- a MASSIVE SHAPE emerges from the
mist... a HORSE- dragging from the stirrup... a DEAD
COP. The rider:

CRANE, IN BURLAP MASK, crown prince of the insane.
Other shapes emerge from the fog behind him, Arkham
INMATES.

> RACHEL
> Crane!

> CRANE
> (shakes head)
> *Scarecrow...*

Filming on BATMAN BEGINS commenced in Iceland in February 2004. The majority of the Himalayan exteriors were shot here on the edge of Vatnajokull Glacier in the southeast of Iceland, the largest glacier in Europe, comprising one tenth of the entire land mass of Iceland.

The glacier moves about four feet daily. Says Liam Neeson, "Christian and I were swordfighting on this ice lake at the foot of this glacier and every so often, between set-ups, we'd see ice crumbling away at the head of the glacier and....you knew that this thing was a big living force that was moving toward you." To the production team, it was important that a real frozen lake be used in order to ensure a full landscape in every shot.

The majority of the other exteriors were shot in Chicago and at Cardington Hangar in Bedfordshire, just north of London. The Chicago streets in the Loop Area, just to the south of the Chicago River, doubled as Gotham City streets, particularly Lower Wacker Drive, where most of the underground car chase scenes were filmed and, very fortuitously, the production was permitted to raise all of the Chicago River bridges in one section of the city for an aerial shot when the Narrows is being cut off from the main island of Gotham City.

For the most part, the majority of other nighttime exteriors were shot at Cardington Hangar. This enormous airship hangar is 160 feet high, 900 feet long and 240 feet wide and is the biggest indoor film set ever created! The Narrows section of Gotham City, a number of city streets and

buildings, the exterior of Arkham Asylum, and the monorail base legs were all constructed and filmed at Cardington. Indeed, a whole section of the city was created here, so vast and detailed that it had street names and working traffic lights, leaving many crew members lost the first few times they wandered around.

In addition, it was an ideal location for special effects. There was huge scope for what could be achieved in terms of wire rigging for Batman to fly, various explosions and steam effects that could be planned and amalgamated into the various buildings as they were constructed. Furthermore, some of the car chases started in Chicago were completed along the 900 feet of constructed road that sometimes had fifty or so cars driving along it.

Another important location was the stately home that doubled as Wayne Manor. Mentmore Towers is situated about an hour and a half north of London, and was built in the 1850s by the Rothschild family. Production Designer Nathan Crowley was immediately drawn to the house. "What's particular about this place is that it has a white interior, so when Bruce returns some years after his parents' deaths, we could really play the white interior as a mausoleum... everything draped and shrouded, and all the carpets rolled up and the white marble floor exposed."

Arkham Asylum plays a very important role within the film and was made up of a number of locations. The main staircase, corridors, and some of the cells were shot at St. Pancras Chambers in London. On October 1, 1868, the first train pulled into the newly built St. Pancras Station in London and a hotel was soon built adjacent to the station. The

built at Cardington based on an exterior that was shot in North London.

A number of scenes were also filmed around University of London buildings, including Senate House in Bloomsbury, where Christopher Nolan and producer Emma Thomas studied and met. The interior and exterior courthouse were all university buildings, and the exterior police station shot where Bruce crouches in the doorway is the entrance to the English Department where Nolan studied.

Perhaps the most interesting of the studio sets that were built for BATMAN BEGINS was the Batcave, which was constructed on a stage at Shepperton Studios near London. The Batcave set was approximately 250 feet long, 120 feet wide and 40 feet high. Twelve water pumps were used to power 12,000 gallons of water that ran

completed building had used 60 million bricks and 9,000 tons of iron work, including polished columns of 14 different types of British granites and limestone. The hotel closed in 1935, was renamed St. Pancras Chambers, and soon became offices. Due for demolition in the 1960s, the building was awarded Grade 1 listed status in recognition of its importance as an example of high Victorian Gothic architecture. For the bath house of the asylum, Abbey Mills Pumping Station in East London was used, and the remainder of the cells were built at Shepperton and Cardington. The exterior at the end of the film (from which the asylum inmates break out) was

through the set every minute in order to create the waterfall, river, and various cave drips. Crowley was keen to show the scale of this natural cavern, with the foundations of the house perched 60 feet above the cave's floor. To this end thousands of sheets cast off existing rocks were bonded together to form the incredible dimensions of the Batcave. Emma Thomas is particularly inspired by this set: "It was a miracle of engineering, quite apart from the scale of it and the beauty and reality of it. It felt so real that you can't imagine it was shot on a stage at Shepperton. It's my favorite set."

As with every other area of filming, director Christopher Nolan wanted the stunts to look real, with a minimum of computer generated enhancement. He explains, "I wanted the action of the film to feel as realistic as possible, and I feel that the use of computers in special effects has very exciting possibilities, but also a lot of pitfalls. I believe that there's a great difference between something that's computer animated, in other words, something that's created on computer from scratch, from something that is shot as far as possible on camera, with stunt performers and special effects that can then be enhanced by computer. The computer is a wonderful tool for compositing and removing wires, rigs, and so forth – but we've tried to use as little animation from scratch as possible, because I feel that the audience will discern the difference between something with a photographic basis, and something that is animated."

One of the earlier major stunts of the film was shot in Iceland, which doubled for the Himalayas. Bruce Wayne flees the burning monastery with Ducard, who has been knocked out. The pair slide down the side of the mountain until Ducard goes over the edge and Bruce catches him. For this stunt, a slide and rigs had to be built, and the stunt doubles, secured by a thin wire, really threw themselves off the edge of the cliff. No mean feat in itself, a techno crane was taken to the top of the glacier where the ice slide had been built so that with a single shot the camera could slide down the ridge and over the edge with the stunt doubles, then tip down to reveal the ravine.

Really bringing Batman's flying action to life was the fact that not only did Batman's stunt double fly on wires, but also film cameras were mounted on wire and followed alongside for maximum effect, with both swooping through the cityscape together. Explains Wally Pfister, the film's director of photography: "You've shot this amazing [footage] of Batman flying 800 feet across a city without the use of visual effects. And that, I think, encapsulates Chris [Nolan's] philosophy of filmmaking, which is, let's do it for real!"

Stunt coordinator Paul Jennings is most proud of one of the most visually spectacular stunts, when Batman falls from the window on fire. With seven cameras trained on him, stunt double Buster Reeves jumped to the ground held by a wire from a fifth story balcony, entirely ablaze. Says Emma Thomas: "It was quite terrifying knowing what Buster was doing for the film. Nothing compares to that kind of dedication. I will never forget seeing him jump out of the fourth story window on fire – it looks spectacular on film."

As expected, the Batmobile was the star attraction in Chicago, where stunt driver George Cottle put the car through its paces as he sped up and down freeways, burst through barriers, and jumped other vehicles. However, perhaps the centerpiece stunt for the Batmobile was its entrance to the Batcave. Of the eight Batmobiles built, there were two lightweight models that did not have engines and these were nitrogen cannoned through the waterfall to land on the floor of the Batcave. The exact duplicate of the working Batmobiles, the stunt ensured that the audience would really see the weight and feel the energy of the vehicle as it blasted through the waterfall – truly an incredible sight.

BATMAN

If they hit the whole city with the toxin, there's no one
to stop Gotham tearing itself apart in mass panic.

INT. MONORAIL TRAIN

Batman SMASHES his gauntlet across Rā's al Ghūl's face- knocking him
aside- forcing him to the floor- Batman grabs Rā's' hair in one hand,
BATARANGS clasped in his fist, steel points protruding like CLAWS,
poised to strike a killing blow...

Rā's looks up at him with scorn...

> RĀ'S AL GHŪL
> Have you finally learned to do what's necessary?

Batman flings the Batarangs at the front windscreen, SHATTERING it...

> BATMAN
> I won't kill you...

Batman pulls a mini-mine from his belt and flings it at the back door,
BLOWING it apart, uncoupling the rear cars... wind HOWLS, FUNNELED
through the train...

> BATMAN (CONT'D)
> *But I don't have to save you...*

Batman's cloak goes RIGID- CATCHES THE WIND- like pulling a rip cord-
Batman is YANKED from Rā's al Ghūl's hands, FLYING BACK THROUGH
THE CAR... AND OUT...

Rā's looks up to see the EXPLODING MONORAIL TOWER ahead...

EXT. MONORAIL STATION

THE TRAIN DERAILS... CRASHING DOWN INTO WAYNE PLAZA- DIGGING
THROUGH THE CONCRETE- METAL SHREDDING, MARBLE SHATTERING,
DUST CLOUDS FLYING, PARKED CARS EXPLODING...

The train has disintegrated into burning rubble just short of the entrance
to Wayne Station...

WAYNE
Batman's just a symbol, Rachel.

Wayne looks confused. Rachel gently brushes
his face with her fingers.

RACHEL
This is your mask. Your real face is
the one criminals now fear. The man
I loved… the man who vanished…
never came back at all.

Wayne stares at her; heartbroken.

RACHEL (CONT'D)
But maybe he's still out there
somewhere. Maybe one day, when
Gotham no longer needs Batman…
I'll see him again.

INT. BOARDROOM,
WAYNE ENTERPRISES

EARLE
Fox, what are you doing here?
I seem to remember firing you.

FOX
You did, but I found a new job.
Yours.

You've started something- bent cops running scared,
hope on the streets...

Gordon leaves his sentence hanging between them.

        BATMAN
        But?

        GORDON
        But there's a lot of weirdness out there right now... the
        Narrows is *lost*... we still haven't picked up Crane or
        half the inmates of Arkham that he freed...

        BATMAN
        We will. Gotham will return to normal.

ACKNOWLEDGEMENTS

The information presented in this book was generously provided by those who worked tirelessly to bring BATMAN BEGINS to the screen. Writing it would not have been possible without access to their knowledge and experience. A large part of 2004 was spent in Gotham City and the world of Batman, a feat of imaginative creation that, amazingly, became my everyday life.

Chris Nolan, David Goyer and Emma Thomas provided essential additional background material - thank you for showing me the bigger picture.

Thank you to Shane Thompson and Irika Slavin at Warner Bros. for their support and advice; to Lisa Blond at New Wave; and to David Cox for his helpful suggestions.

And love to Jeremy, Giles and Antony - my own personal super heroes.

SPECIAL THANKS

David James, John J. Hill, Chris Cerasi, Georg Brewer, Steve Korté, Matthew Denk, Manny Jose, Barbara Rich, Susannah Scott, Mick Mayhew, Melissa Miller, Shawn Knapp, Bozena Bannett, Alexandra Bliss, Glenn Buonocore, Bernadette Corbie, Suzanne Janso, Robert Marasco, Brooke McGuire, Adriana Tierno

Time Inc. Home Entertainment

Publisher   Richard Fraiman

Executive Director, Marketing Services   Carol Pittard

Director, Retail & Special Sales   Tom Mifsud

Marketing Director, Branded Businesses   Swati Rao

Director, New Product Development   Peter Harper

Assistant Financial Director   Steven Sandonato

Prepress Manager   Emily Rabin

Product Manager   Victoria Alfonso

Book Production Manager   Jonathan Polsky

Associate Prepress Manager   Anne-Michelle Gallero

Published by Time Inc. Home Entertainment

Time Inc. 1271 Avenue of the Americas   New York, New York 10020

All rights reserved. No part of this book may be reproduced in any form or by any electronic
or mechanical means, including information storage and retrieval systems, without permission
in writing from the publisher, except by a reviewer, who may quote brief passages in a review.

Page 12/13: Art from *Batman: The Dark Knight Returns* by Frank Miller and Klaus Janson; art
from *Batman: The Long Halloween* by Tim Sale; art from *Detective Comics #27* by Bob Kane.

Pages 14/15: Text from *Batman: Year One* by Frank Miller, art by David Mazzucchelli.

ISBN: 1-932273-44-1

Time Inc. Home Entertainment is a subsidiary of Time Inc.

If you would like to order any of our hardcover Collector's Edition books, please call us at

1-800-327-6388. (Monday through Friday, 7:00 a.m.— 8:00 p.m. or Saturday,

7:00 a.m.— 6:00 p.m. Central Time).

GORDON

I never said thank-you.

BATMAN

And you'll never have to.